I0668162

Diary

of a

Wish Fairy

Story and Illustrations by

Linda Sobel

Text and Illustrations Copyright © 2016 Linda Sobel

Cover Art Copyright © 2016 J. Lynn Howell

Editing and Design by Sarla V. J. Matsumura

All Rights Reserved

Library of Congress Control Number: 2016918582

ISBN-13: 978-0692780398
ISBN-10: 0692780394

Published by Lavender Sky Press, West Shokan, New York

DEDICATION

To all the children. I wish you the best.

To Beth Hin and Charlotte Smith for their constant
inspiration and support.

To Cazzy, the wonder dog, my wish puppy, who started
me on this book decades ago.

And to my beloved husband, Joe Ferrara, who not only
supports my every dream but keeps me grounded
on the planet.

JUNE 18

I did it! I passed every class and graduated from Fairy College.

As we lined up to receive our diplomas, a cloud of butterflies suddenly appeared and filled the air. The sunlight bouncing off their wings formed a dizzying kaleidoscope of colors.

Without warning, the butterflies massed over my head. They merged into a rotating silver and gold vortex that soared high into the sky, flashed brighter than the sun, then vanished.

Everyone spoke at once.

"I've never, ever, seen anything like that."

"An omen for sure."

"Was that a special message for someone?"

Dazzled, I remained in line and flew slowly to the stage. Professor Candle waited, hands fluttering at her sides. When I reached her, a diploma materialized in the air and my name appeared in perfect calligraphy.

"Congratulations," she said, "I knew you'd make it."

My parents were so proud of me. Not everyone has what it takes to be a wish fairy, especially a birthday wish fairy.

But can I do it? What if I fail and ruin a child's birthday wish?

I have mixed feelings and doubts, and yet, I can't wait for the birthday parties to begin.

JUNE 19

Birdsong woke me before dawn. I leapt out of my bed of soft thistle down and flew around the room. I stopped suddenly. Would my first birthday party be today? How do I find out? Would the message come by snailmail or dragonfly racer? I remembered the words of Professor Candle, "The first contact will be a surprise."

I relaxed and went outside.

Home was a hollow, high in an oak tree, about fifteen feet off the ground. I like to be elevated, to view the meadow and the comings and goings of all of her creatures.

Just below the door, a large woody mushroom jutted out from the tree trunk. This was my porch and the reason I'd chosen this particular tree as home.

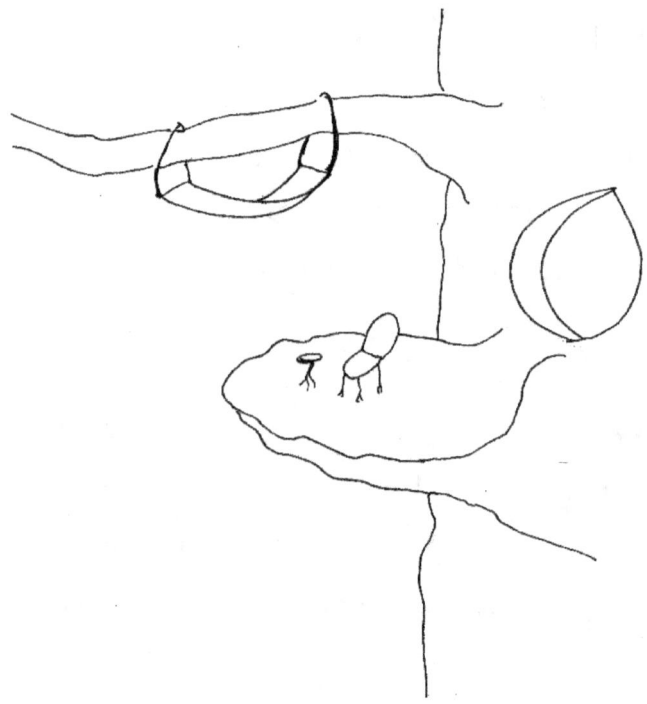

As I sat and drank my morning cup of honeysuckle tea, Jewel darted at my face. I gently swatted her away and she flew toward the open doorway.

"Follow me," she said.

Jewel's turquoise and purple wings looked like wind-blown flower petals. Although small, she was super fast for a dragonfly and I could not keep up with her.

A small mirror had appeared on the dining room wall.

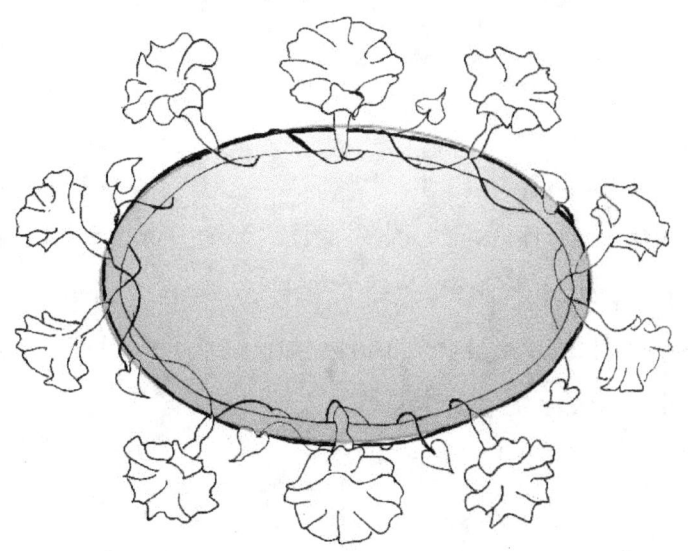

As I approached it, words started to scroll down from the top:

Congratulations!
I am the work assignment mirror. Your first party will be on June 25. Relax, and have a fun week.
Sparky

The second I finished reading the mirror, it shrank into the size of a compact mirror. That was it? Where was the party? What time was it? And who was Sparky?

JUNE 20

I still know nothing about the time and place of my first birthday party. What am I to do? What if I don't find out in time and I'm late or I miss the party completely?

I caught myself. What's happening to me? I'm a fairy and fairies don't worry. We're never late. I remembered Professor Candle's mantra, "Trust life and the unfolding of events. Everything in its own time."

I took a deep breath and inhaled the heady perfume of wild roses and trumpet lilies. I called Jewel and we flew to the pond to meet the newly opened flowers of the morning.

Close to the shore, a large blue flag iris had just opened. The upper petals were silver in the morning sunlight and the lower petals were a deep blue dusted with drops of dew. Instantly, I imagined the flower transformed into a dress. The bodice was a silvery satin and the skirt was a blue chiffon accented with silver beads. Satin reflects light, while chiffon is as light as air and won't weigh me down when I fly.

Imagining something is the first step. I closed my eyes and pictured the dress in every detail. I envisioned the gentle drape of the skirt, the luxurious feeling of the fabric against my skin, and the beads catching and reflecting the light.

I fluttered my wings, nodded my head once, and commanded, "Become."

The air moved as the dress appeared and glided over my body. It was perfect. I'll wear it to my first birthday party.

June 22

While passing through my dining room, I discovered that the mirror had grown. At last, a message! I flew closer and these words appeared:

Stephen's 8th Birthday
June 25, 1:00 PM
331 Bluebird Circle
Sparky

A detailed aerial map showed the location of the party.

Suddenly, an image of a boy hovered in front of the mirror. My first birthday boy. Oh, Sparky, thank you. Another mystery solved.

June 25

Today's the day. My wings quivered. Yes, I was definitely nervous. Could I do it? Could I hear the birthday wish of a human child? I had practiced at the college with my friends. I could hear their wishes loud and clear. But fairies vibrate at a higher frequency than children. After three long years of studying how to silence my mind and open my listening heart to the wish of a child, I hoped I was prepared. What if I couldn't hear the birthday wish? I trembled at the thought.

I remembered the words of Professor Candle. "Your complete focus is the birthday wish. Stay alert for the birthday cake. It usually appears when the children are seated around a table. But some parents like to whisk the cake out and surprise the Birthday Child. In the beginning you may need a few minutes to get ready. As soon as you see that cake with flaming candles, stop moving, slow your breathing, and quiet your mind. Have no expectations. Open your listening heart."

In my excitement I arrived a few minutes early and found a living room filled with a pack of screaming, fidgeting children.

A group of guests circled a blindfolded boy who staggered around the room holding a paper tail with a thumbtack.

They shouted conflicting directions at the same time.

"Turn right!"

"Go straight."

"Too high."

The chaotic energy swirled around the room like a mini hurricane. Overwhelmed, I flew backward until the edges of my wings brushed the wall.

A loud clapping noise frightened me. The wall shook. I turned and saw the birthday boy slamming his hand against a poster of a tailless donkey.

I flew closer to observe him.

Just then, the blindfolded boy bumped into a low table. He fell backward with a cry and grabbed his knee.

Stephen ran over to his injured guest. He gently removed the blindfold and helped his friend up.

"It's OK. You don't have to play anymore. My mother suggested this game," he said. "Let's eat." He nudged his friend in the direction of a large table.

Good idea, I thought.

I followed the boys to the table and tasted human food for the first time. Pizza, I love pizza. It's such a wonderful, gooey way to eat cheese and tomatoes. The number of treats was staggering: chocolates, nuts, jelly beans, cupcakes, cookies, pretzels, corn chips, sweet potato chips, and cheese strings.

I flew to a plate of cookies, broke off a piece, and tasted it. The exploding sweetness of a chocolate chip cookie charged my body. At that exact moment, a girl reaching for a cookie stared right at me and pulled her hand back in surprise. Oh no, I had become visible!

Too late, I remembered Professor Candle's caution, "We are invisible to 99.9% of all humans. Only a teeny 0.1% believe in us and are open to seeing all aspects of creation. But if you eat too much party food, your body will become denser. Make sure they don't see you!" she emphasized.

I slowed my breathing, changed my vibration, and went invisible again.

Wow, that warning was for real. I will always remember this.

A bright light caught my eye. I spun around quickly and saw my first birthday cake. The birthday candles flickered as the cake was carried into the room.

This is it, my first birthday wish. My heart pounded.

I hovered behind Stephen's left ear and waited. He closed his eyes and started blowing out the candles. After the third try, I did as I was taught and helped him blow them out. At the same time, I listened inwardly and heard his wish. "I want a puppy." I even saw the breed. It was a golden retriever.

I did it! I heard the wish! What a relief.

June 26

How do I fulfill my first birthday wish?

I returned to Stephen's house and found his father, Paul, reading the morning paper. While looking over Paul's shoulder, I quickly scanned the classified section. When I spotted an ad for golden retriever puppies, I fanned my wings and the pages flipped to that section.

Paul placed his hand firmly on the paper to hold it down. He started reading. I focused my attention and highlighted the puppy ad with a soft iridescent glow. He read it! I did it. I planted the idea. This was too easy.

I congratulated myself and took the rest of the day off as the temperature soared into the mid 90's.

I followed Jewel to the pond. We lay down on a lily pad and watched the clouds float by.

June 27

I wondered, did the boy get his wish puppy? I returned to Stephen's house. No puppy!

What went wrong?

In the evening, when the day's energy quieted, I broadcasted a fairy search to all dogs within a thirty-mile radius of the birthday boy's house.

Remembering that it is always polite to start a message with a pleasant salutation, I started with "It's a beautiful evening. I am a Birthday Wish Fairy in need of a golden retriever puppy."

I waited for a response.

"My babies are pure bred golden retrievers. Five of them still need a home," said the mother golden of the classified ad.

"I highlighted that ad for your sweet ones, but the father never acted on it," I told her.

I wished her good luck in finding homes for her babies, said goodbye, and listened to the other messages.

Suddenly I had a plan.

June 28

At the end of the workday, I waited on the roof of Paul's car. When he opened the door, I quickly slipped inside, careful not to brush against him. I made sure that I stayed invisible and off we went.

He merged onto the highway and went east through the business district. It was time to act. Two miles before the exit, his car developed a loud knocking noise. A mile later, the car started to buck. He hastily exited the highway looking for help.

"Keep going," I urged him quietly from the back seat.

He drove into the first service station he found and turned the car off. "I hope the mechanic is still here," he said to himself.

Yes! This is the place. My plan is working. I was thrilled.

Paul walked into an empty office, looked around and continued into the shop. He found the mechanic with his head buried under the hood of an old black pickup truck.

"Hello! Can you look at my car?" he asked. "Suddenly it's making strange noises and bucking."

"I'm just about done here," the mechanic mumbled. He emerged from under the hood of the pickup truck and wiped his oily hands on a rag. "Let me take it for a drive."

"I'll wait here," Paul said, tossing the keys to the mechanic.

I closed my eyes and inhaled the metallic, oily smell of the garage. My nose crinkled. But floating over the fumes was the sweet essence of puppy. Where were they?

I sent out a message to the mother dog. "I'm here. I can feel you, but I can't see you. Where are you?"

"Look in the corner behind the tools," she said.

I flew behind the tool box and saw her. A dab of oil stained her tan and brown coat, but her bed was spotless. Eight puppies ranging from dark brown to pale gold were sleeping by her side.

"They're all different colors," I said.

"Their father is a pure bred golden retriever. His blonde coat is lighter than mine. He is very handsome and very kind," the mother dog replied.

"Can you wake them?" I asked.

"First you must tell me about the boy," she commanded.

"He buzzes with energy, but he's also very sweet. When he made his wish, I felt his love."

"You're a Wish Fairy. I trust your intuition."

She gently nosed her babies and woke them up. They went from a deep sleep, to yawning, to pouncing on each other in less than a minute. She lifted one puppy by the scruff of his neck, set him on the floor and licked his face.

"This one looks just like his father. And he is full of mischief. A sweet, energetic boy would be ideal for him," she said.

"He looks exactly like the boy's wish puppy. He's perfect," I said.

She pushed the puppy in Paul's direction. He looked like a furry truck with large bones, huge paws, and amber headlight eyes. He scampered over to the man and pulled his pants leg.

"Hey there buddy, where did you come from?"

Paul bent over and lifted the puppy onto his lap. The puppy's tail spun around in a fast circle as he squirmed in the man's arms and licked his entire face.

"Whoa, you're a sweetie. You remind me of someone I used to know when I was a boy," he said with a faraway look in his eyes. He sat on the chair and firmly held the wriggling puppy.

The shop door opened and the mechanic returned. "No noise, no bucking, nothing." He shook his head and tossed back the keys. "You found the puppies, I see."

"No, he found me," Paul said, planting a little kiss on the dog's head. "Does he need a home? My boy turned eight this week and I want to surprise him with a puppy. It's time for him to have a dog."

"If you promise to give him a good home, you can have him," the mechanic said with a smile.

Phew! I breathed a sigh of relief. Mission accomplished.

July 6

I'm having a blast. This past weekend I went to five birthday parties, three on Saturday and two on Sunday. The variety of games astounded me: board games, ball games, and games of make believe.

And the birthday cakes! In one weekend I tasted carrot cake, chocolate mousse cake with slivered almonds, angel food cake, and ice-cream cake. One party had a soccer ball cake with white icing on the outside and chocolate cake on the inside. I love my job. I get to wear fabulous outfits, go to parties, and eat cake.

July 11

I never knew that birthday parties came in so many forms: surprise parties, bowling parties, swimming parties, and pajama parties. Who knows what's next?

One day when dashing from a swimming party to a bowling party, I dripped water on the bowling alley and the birthday boy slipped into the bowling alley gutter. The sudden appearance of water on the bowling lane surprised everyone.

I dried myself quickly by creating a breeze with my wings. The air conditioning raised goose bumps on my entire body. Fairies don't like to be cold and wet.

It's a challenge going from party to party. There is barely enough time to make it from one birthday cake to the next and I like to be properly clothed in order to participate in the theme of each party. I never know if I'm attending an indoor or outdoor party, a wet or a dry party.

I wonder if the assignment mirror could list the theme of the birthday party. That would be so helpful. While jumping from party to party, I could instantly fashion a new outfit and be prepared for anything.

Thank goodness the birthday boy did not get hurt.

July 13

Today, as I stood in front of the assignment mirror, I wondered, "Does this thing work both ways? Can I get a message to Sparky?"

I reached out to examine the mirror. As soon as my finger touched it, the mirror grew and a piece of light blue chalk hovered in the air.

I grabbed the chalk and wrote a question,

Is it possible to know the theme of each birthday party?

Sparky wrote back,

I need to dress appropriately,

Why?

I answered.

Sparky replied,

What difference does it
make? You're invisible.

I answered,

It matters to me.

Sparky,

You're a fairy. Fashion an outfit. Remember the dress you made at the pond? That was a classic.

Sparky was not helpful. He never answered my question and how did he know about my dress?

July 16

Another party.

Carla's 4th Birthday
July 17, 1:00
124 Castle Rd
Dress Fancy
Sparky

A pale blue light streamed out of the mirror. A young girl was lovingly dressing her dolls. She picked one up and said, "Tomorrow is my party. You have to be ready."

July 17

Today's party transported me into a child's fantasy. Brightly colored streamers hung from the ceiling. The living room had tiny tables with matching chairs and table linens. Doll-sized cups and saucers covered every surface.

As each guest entered the room, the mom immediately swathed her in a sparkling shawl and showered her with golden sprinkles. Sparkles of excitement radiated out of each girl's aura. I bathed in the flickering lights and shared the sensation of wonder that danced around the room. The girls were so open, so ready to experience this celebration. I leapt into the mood of the party.

The cake, decorated with little dolls and pink icing had chocolate mousse with raspberries on the inside. Carla squeezed her eyes shut and made her wish. "I wish I had a baby sister to dress up."

I don't think I can do anything about that wish.

July 23

Today, just when the birthday girl inhaled to blow out the candles, her mother whispered in her ear. "Don't spit on it!"

But it wasn't a whisper. Everyone heard it and laughed. The birthday girl's eyes glistened with unshed tears. I breathed into her ear, "They aren't laughing at you. Parents often embarrass their children. They don't mean to, it happens all the time."

She sighed, took a deep breath, and with a mighty whoosh, blew out the candles. I'm sorry to say that the cake did get a little wet, but no one noticed.

August 1

Life is so busy. How do I balance work, have time for friends, and take care of my home?

The sink is filled with piles of dishes, dust bunnies float in every room, and the flower garden is full of weeds. This is the first time I've lived alone and have been responsible for everything. How do my parents do it?

Time to get to work. I flew through the house and imagined it spotless. I pictured every room in great detail, gleaming floors, a neatly made bed, and a sparkling kitchen.

I fluttered my wings, nodded my head once, and commanded, "Sparkling clean."

The air moved. Every surface glistened. That felt better.

I flew outside to my flower garden and looked at the jungle of weeds. It was disrespectful to just pull plants without a discussion. They had a right to live and a reason for choosing certain spots to grow.

"Attention ladies," I said. "I know that you love it here, but you are crowding my flowers and they need more room. Any suggestions?"

The little chickweeds, covered with tiny white star flowers answered, "We came here because you need us.

Throw us in your salads or juice us. Then there will be plenty of room for everyone."

The chickweeds spoke the truth. During the month of July, I hadn't prepared proper meals. Instead, I stashed my wing pockets with party food to eat later. My complexion has changed and not for the better. I broke out in blemishes and have lost the healthy moonlight glow that emanates from a fairy's skin. Even though the children can't see me, I am visible to all fairies, plants, and most animals. I don't like spots on my face. It's not fitting for a fairy.

August 5

The mirror had a message.

Jake's 6th Birthday
August 6, 2:00
77 Thunder Rd
Sparky

The blue light of the mirror projected a young boy with short dark hair and angry eyes. His mother stood next to him, rubbing his shoulder, trying to calm him down.

I got the chills and wondered if I could handle this party.

August 6

A pack of screaming five and six year old boys ruled the house. Ignoring the planned games, they made one up.

"Follow me," Jake yelled.

He ran through the house, banging on walls and swiping at things on tables. The other boys followed him. Books fell off shelves and little animal statues went flying. A large framed photograph shattered as it hit the tile floor.

"Stand back," shouted Jake's mother. "Don't anyone move."

She ran into the kitchen and returned with a whiskbroom and a dustpan. After the glass shards were collected and dumped into the trash she vacuumed the floor.

"Into the dining room, everyone, and sit down," Jake's mother ordered. "If you're standing, no ice cream cake. That's the rule."

She gritted her teeth and ran into the kitchen for the cake.

Yes, bring the cake. I could not wait to leave this party of hooligans.

When the cake was set in front of Jake, I perched on his shoulder and waited for the wish.

Suddenly, from out of nowhere, a spoon went flying. It bounced off the boy's head and hit my tiara. The tiara fell to the floor and broke into three pieces. I gathered the pieces, turned them into a crash helmet, placed that on my head and returned to the boy's shoulder just in time for the birthday wish.

He closed his eyes. "I want a dump truck."
He blew out the candles.

Instantly I saw it, a blue dump truck.
That should be no problem.

Before his wish had faded, I was back
at my pond, floating on a lily pad.

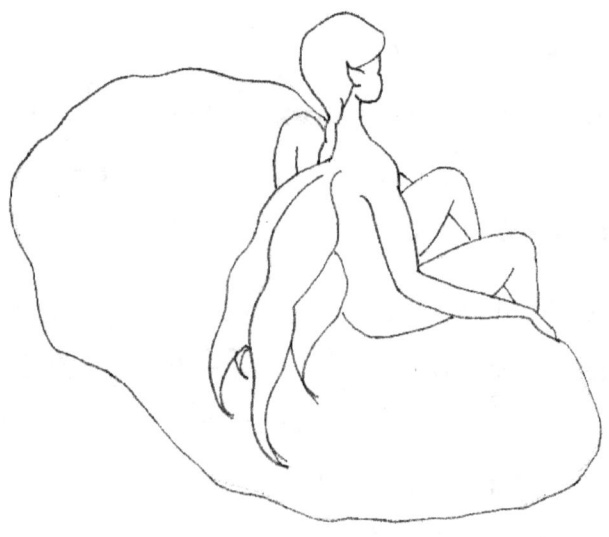

August 7

In *Gift Creation* class, we practiced making and dissolving toys. The Fairy Workshop was purposely built over a creative energy vortex. We could make toys appear or disappear within seconds.

Wanting to be free of the wild party assignment, I arrived at the Fairy Workshop just after sunrise.

I found a quiet corner, closed my eyes, and imagined the blue dump truck in every detail.

I fluttered my wings, nodded my head, once and commanded, "Become."

When I opened my eyes, a blue dump truck with a red hood stood before me.

I goofed!

I dissolved the red hood, watched the red particles get sucked into the energy vortex, then imagined a blue one. Perfect!

I pictured the truck gift wrapped, boxed, and addressed to Jake. The sender would remain a mystery.

August 9

I wondered, did the package arrive safely? I returned to Jake's house and saw the dump truck in the yard.

I flew closer. The truck lay broken and abandoned. The doors were dented and all four wheels were missing.

Why did Jake break his toy? Why is he so angry?

Saddened I flew home.

August 11

When I was in school I used to love dusk. The waning light mutes and softens the landscape. Now when Evening Star first shows herself, I have no peace. Children's wishes pop up faster than microwave popcorn and within a five mile radius I can hear them. All of them.

But why am I hearing these wishes? They aren't birthday wishes. Are they part of my job?

I remembered the words of Professor Cosmo, "Creation can show herself a little at a time or all at once. It all depends on your state of receptivity. Be open to the mystery. Pay attention."

But why am I hearing these wishes?

August 18

I watched the mirror expand.

> *Lara's 12th Birthday*
>
> *August 20, 1:00*
>
> *720 Willow Lane*
>
> *Sparky*

The mirror showed a young girl skipping through a field, swinging a basket. She was singing nonsense rhymes to her calico cat who followed her like a dog.

Suddenly the mirror shrunk, then with a whoosh, expanded again

Felicity's 14th Birthday
August 20, 5:00
233 Central Ave
Sparky

The mirror projected a young teenager dressed in tight black jeans, a red tank top, and platform shoes.

Two parties coming up.

August 20

Today's first party made my heart sing. This family believed in fairies and expected me! How did they know I was coming?

They prepared a small basket filled with gifts that fairies love: beads of all sizes and shapes, brightly colored pieces of glass, and sparkling, iridescent crystals.

Next to the table, perched on an empty birdbath, the family fashioned a tiny throne draped in richly embroidered fabrics and covered with garlands of flowers. This thoughtful welcome brought tears to my eyes. I never realized that I needed to be acknowledged for the work that I do.

As I moved around the backyard, Lara kept looking in my direction. Could she see me? I gasped a little and felt a wondrous smile split my face. I smoothed my sparkly lavender dress and adjusted my beaded headpiece.

A rainbow of colors floated into the room. Daylilies, nasturtium, and Johnny

Jump-Ups made an edible flower garden on top of the birthday cake.

I placed myself behind Lara and waited. She closed her eyes.

From deep within her heart, I heard, "I wish I could understand what plants are feeling when I talk to them."

Wow, what a profound wish. I gave a little spin of joy.

But this wish was out of my realm of experience. I will have to get a message to Professor Pan who taught *Plant Languages & Communication* at the Fairy College. Perhaps he will assign a special fairy to teach Lara how to communicate with the plant kingdom.

What a great time. My whole body was smiling.

August 20

Applying makeup dominated the second party. The girls practiced for hours with blush, eyeliner, and lipstick.

In spite of the giggling, something about this party disturbed me. A current of unease vibrated through the room and I couldn't figure out why. My feelings were confirmed when Felicity made her wish.

"I wish that Jennifer would spill blush powder all over herself. Then she won't be so popular. She'll look ridiculous."

I watched, stunned. I couldn't move or act. Professor Candle's voice played in my head, "Do nothing with a hurtful wish. Let the Universe take care of it."

It never made any sense to me before, but now, feeling it, I knew that I could never take action on a wish like that. It made my heart ache.

Minutes after the wish, Felicity inexplicably dropped her cake. It fell in slow motion. The chocolate icing smeared her embroidered blouse and splattered her batik skirt.

The Universe works fast. Professor Candle knows her stuff.

August 21

I awoke to a hot, muggy day.

I called Jewel and we raced to the pond. I nestled in the shade of a water lily and dangled my feet in the water.

"Why are you so quiet? Is something wrong?" Jewel asked.

"It's the birthday parties. Nothing is as I expected. Earlier this month I made a wonderful blue dump truck in the Fairy Workshop and mailed it to the birthday boy. When I checked to make sure it arrived, I found it broken and abandoned in the boy's yard."

My wings drooped as I remembered the feeling.

"There is more. Yesterday, I went to two parties. They expected me at the first one. I sat on a throne and was gifted with treasures. It was wonderful. I felt so validated, so loved.

But at the second party, the birthday girl made a wish to humiliate one of her guests. I felt the pain of it in my heart. It still hurts."

I rubbed my chest.

"I'm wondering if I made the right choice about being a wish fairy. I thought that making birthday wishes come true was important and that I would be happy. I am not so sure any more."

I peered into the water and was surprised to see a drawn face staring back at me.

"I really thought I was making a difference," I wailed.

"Things aren't always what they seem, but there is always the journey," Jewel said.

I moaned. "Not another one of your vague and puzzling statements."

"What do you expect? I'm wise in the ways of dragonflies," Jewel replied. Suddenly Jewel flew into my shoulder and knocked me into the water. We spent the rest of the morning playing tag with the water spiders.

September 10

Summer was a whirlwind with parties any day of the week. Now the children are back in school and the weather has cooled down. No more swimming parties. I preferred the lake parties where no stinging chlorine burned my eyes. A few times I found new wildflowers to admire and befriend. I miss working outdoors.

The horseback riding party topped my list of favorites. I clung to the birthday boy's shirt and enjoyed a wild ride through the woods.

The mare kept turning back and grinning because she knew the birthday boy could not see me.

September 15

I'm overworked and exhausted. I never thought I would feel this way. I imagined a job filled with parties would never be boring or stressful, that it would always be fun. There are always new kids, new games, and endless food. But, it's not always sweetness and puppy dog wishes. Some of the kids are just plain mean.

September 17

Today's birthday party bewildered me.

At the time of the birthday candles, when everyone's focus was on the birthday boy, I heard a whisper of a wish from one of the guests.

"I wish I had a best friend."

Then she let her attention wander from her wish back to the birthday boy and the cake.

She forgot her wish! I was shocked that she gave it no significance. It seemed to me that she barely heard it.

I can't stop asking myself. Why did I hear her wish?

September 19

I can't stop thinking about that girl and her wish. I watched the energy of that wish jump from her heart onto the silver web that connects all of Life. Within seconds, all of Creation felt it.

Does she realize what she has set into motion? Does she know that Creation hears every wish and aligns to answer that wish?

I'm still confused and don't know what to do because this unexpected wish raises many questions for me. I heard her wish, but she was not the birthday child. Do I have a responsibility to grant her wish? My job is to help birthday wishes come true.

How many wishes have I missed because I was too busy watching the party games and tasting new treats?

I remembered the words of Professor Cosmo, "Be ready for anything. We live in a multi-leveled reality in this finely woven universe."

October 1

I feel that I am missing a very important part of my job. I know the importance of Traditional Times to Make a Wish. That was drummed into us at school.

Topping the list is birthdays. The birthday cake ritual makes sure that children have a scheduled time each year to make a wish. There is often a quiet pause between the arrival of the cake and making the wish.

But birthday wishes are usually spontaneous. Most of the time, they are not taken seriously. Some children seem surprised that they have to make a wish. Others are so desperate for cake that they rush through their wish. Often there is screaming and pushing. The sugar overload makes some of them wild. I know what one bite of one cookie did to me.

October 2

I tried an experiment at today's birthday party. I ignored the games and grabbed just one cookie. I sat quietly in the corner and listened. It took time to tune out the noise of the party.

The drooling dog wished for a plate of cake à la mode to fall on the floor. His wish worked! As soon as that plate hit the floor, the dog ran over, and slurped it clean.

October 9

The most amazing thing happened at today's party. Not only did I hear a quiet wish, I saw it. It was a wish to be loved and it was pink. It floated out of a little girl's heart, hovered in front of her, and blended into the space around her.

I was dumbfounded. I was taught to concentrate on the Birthday Wish.

But just then, I remembered the class, *The Universe and Its Mysteries.* Professor Cosmo had said, "Be open to the dance of life. Creation shows herself in infinite ways. Stay open to see what the Universe will reveal."

October 12

I keep seeing that little pink wish. Where did it come from? Not from the birthday girl.

Is there another category of wishes I know nothing about? Are they more or less important than the wishes on the Traditional List? What about other children's wishes? How do I find the answers to my questions?

I have decided to eat before I arrive at a birthday party and pay no attention to the games. This will allow me to take care of the Birthday Wish and be on the alert for other wishes.

October 29

Donna's 15th Birthday
October 31, 7:30
7092 Washington Avenue
Sparky

October 31

Everyone wore full costumes with makeup and masks. Sparky sent me a picture of a young teenager with frizzy brown hair and dark brown eyes. But I couldn't find her.

To add to the confusion, mobs of kids continually approached the house and yelled, "Trick or Treat." They held out shopping bags overflowing with candy and begged for more.

No snacks for me. I had to find the birthday girl. I found a girl about the right height, with similar brown eyes, but she had long straight black hair.

My heart pounded. Where was Donna?

What if I missed the birthday cake and the birthday wish? Of course, the cake! The birthday cake will lead me to Donna.

I waited by the kitchen door. It was hard to wait and do nothing. No game watching and no snacking.

A boring 20 minutes later, Donna's mom carried an orange and black birthday cake out of the kitchen. Plastic ghosts and witches topped the orange icing. I followed it into the dining room. She placed the cake in front of the girl with the long black hair. The birthday girl had disguised herself with a wig.

I perched on the girl's shoulder and waited. She scrunched her eyes closed and made her wish.

"I wish I had straight hair."

With a mighty exhale she blew out every candle.

What can I do about that wish? I'm not allowed to straighten her hair. Or am I? I just don't know.

November 13

I thought that I had today off, but when I passed through the dining room, a tall boy with curly shoulder length hair hovered in front of the mirror.

Dakota's 15th Birthday
TODAY, 12:00 Noon
Skateboard Court
Sorry, This party was
planned at the last minute.
Thanks, Sparky

I sped through my household chores and dashed off to the party. When I arrived the boys were whooping and hollering as each one took a turn with his skateboard on the steep ramps.

Dakota awed everyone. He pushed off the top and quickly picked up speed. He flew over the edge of the ramp and twisted around in two complete circles. Then Dakota zoomed back down the ramp and up the other side to complete his turn.

I have never seen anything like it. I wonder if fairies would consider this sport. With our wings, we could bring skateboarding to new heights.

I watched boy after boy practice his skills with the skateboard.

Finally, it was time for the cake, and what a cake. It was a large chocolate skateboard with cupcake wheels.

Dakota closed his eyes, waited, and made his wish.

"I wish I had a snowboard. Then I'd be so cool."

I saw the wish. Dakota stood on a mountaintop, holding a new snowboard. His turquoise jacket, two sizes too large for him, sagged over baggy pants.

Cool? I thought that he was already cool, so independent and sure of himself. And he could skateboard like he had wings. I admit that I wasn't too crazy about the outfit in his wish, but what did I know about boys' fashion?

Those loose snowboard clothes do nothing for me.

But I can't help but wonder, can a snowboard make someone cool?

November 20

I am relieved that I am not a Holiday Fairy. Thanksgiving would be exhausting.

Traditionally, the kids always get the wishbone. With my luck, I'd hear every wish. Imagine Thanksgiving and hundreds of wishbones snapping at the same time. Absolutely impossible!

I will let the Holiday Wish Fairies take care of those wishes.

December 17

There has been a lull in the birthday parties. I haven't heard from Sparky since before Thanksgiving. I wonder why? Is it possible that there are no birthday parties? Good, I need a break.

December 21

Today all the fairies of the Home Forest met at dusk to celebrate the Winter Solstice. From this day until the Summer Solstice in June, more sunlight will warm the Earth and catapult us into the growing seasons of spring and summer. I hope to discover new flowers to inspire new dress designs.

I couldn't wait to see my friends. But first I had to eat.

A feast of dishes crowded a low log. For my main course, I chose a large slice of acorn squash pie mixed with ground nuts and seasoned with herbs. I loaded wild rice on the side and was thrilled to see a winter green salad. Someone had traveled to the Secret Cove hidden in a faraway valley and gathered fresh greens.

For dessert, I selected dried flower blossoms brushed lightly with honey and sprinkled with saffron. This was a delicacy, even by fairy standards.

I found a comfortable seat on a small rock and surprised myself by devouring the salad first.

At that moment, North Wind blew through the crowd and a paper floated onto my plate and stuck to the honeyed flowers. I looked up in dismay and there was an older fairy, balancing a plate heaped with food, trying to catch loose pages that swirled in every direction.

I put my plate down, quickly gathered as many papers as I could, and approached him. His curly hair stuck out in all directions. He looked familiar. Where had I seen him?

"I think I got them all except for the one that's stuck to my dessert," I said.

I handed him the pages, then flew back to my plate and pulled the paper off my now crushed dessert. It was sticky with honey. I glanced at it, planning to lick off the honey, and saw a list of names, dates, and ages.

"What is this?" I asked him.

"I'm working on next year's birthday party assignments. I know that it's ridiculous to use paper, but I am old fashioned. Sparky, at your service," he said with a graceful aerial bow.

"I knew you looked familiar. Didn't you visit Professor Candle's class a few weeks before graduation?"

"Yes. I meet all the graduating Wish Fairies. It helps me enormously with the party assignments."

"I'm . . .," I started to say.

"I know who you are," Sparky said. "I know everyone. It's part of my job."

He stacked the papers on a large flat rock, covered them with another rock and attacked his food.

We sat quietly and ate. Within minutes Sparky's plate was empty. He turned to me.

"It was a pleasure to share a meal with you. I must go. Another year of birthday parties will soon be upon us."

He grabbed the papers, bowed, and was gone.

I finished eating and searched for my friends. I flew over and caught the tail end of a conversation.

"I worked a birthday at a large toy store. The guests had fifteen minutes to find a party favor and bring it to the cash register. No price limit. Cake was never served at this party," Misty said.

"My last birthday party broke out in a food fight. Have you ever see one? They threw food at each other and smeared whipped cream on their faces. I loved it," Rocky said.

Food fights, nasty wishes, more toys. These stories depressed me. Party after party, cake after cake, wish after wish. Is this to be the story of my life?

Rocky was backlit by the warm colors of the solstice fire. I tuned out the conversation. The fire was calling me.

I flew closer to watch the dancing flames of orange, red, and blue.

I felt a deep yearning for something, but I had no idea what.

December 23

Kirsten's 12th Birthday

December 24, 4:00

709 Cardinal Lane

Sparky

A young preteen hovered in front of the mirror. She had short, short red hair and piercing light gray eyes.

December 24

Curiosity propelled me to arrive early because I've never seen the inside of a house decorated for the holiday season.

Strings of multicolored lights wrapped the shrubs and the evergreen trees, while sparkling lights outlined the roof, the chimney, and the walkway. A pinecone wreath adorned the front door and electric candles warmed all the windows.

A huge Christmas tree brightened and perfumed the family room. I inhaled the wonderful energy of a living tree. This was a very happy Christmas tree, still growing in a big pot of soil. Piles of brightly wrapped presents surrounded the tree. Five enormous stockings stuffed with candy and presents hung on the fireplace mantle. An embroidered name embellished each stocking.

I found the party in the dining room. Ten girls were seated around the table eating tiny red and green hors d'oeuvres. They did not look appetizing.

A stack of presents was piled in front of Kirsten. She examined the boxes and scowled.

I could hear her thoughts.

"This is the worst day for a birthday. Every year I get cheated in presents and some of them are even wrapped in Christmas paper. This is never a special day just for me. Everyone gets presents this time of year."

Out of the corner of my eye I saw the birthday cake coming through the door. It was decorated with Santa's elves. Oh no, she will not be happy with this cake.

I slowed my breathing and listened for the birthday wish.

"It's not fair. My sister's birthday is in March and mine is on Christmas Eve. I wish that I had a June birthday."

Poof, she blew out every candle on the first try.

I never realized there were so many wasted wishes.

January 12

Mark's 14th Birthday
January 14, 3:00
15 York Place
Sparky
Be alert!

The birthday boy's image hovered in front of the mirror. Green eyes, glasses, and black hair.

Alert for what?

January 14

Today's party confused me. The party was split into two distinct arenas and I had trouble finding the birthday boy. Sparky sent me a picture of a boy with black curly hair, green eyes, and glasses.

First I looked downstairs. Cloaked and masked boys filled the basement family room. They whacked each other with plastic swords and yelled, "Run him through, don't let him get away! He betrayed the king."

I saw a masked boy with green eyes and black hair, but no glasses. The birthday boy must be in the other group. This was a new one. I'd never seen a group of guests playing without the birthday child.

The noise from upstairs bounced off the walls and deafened me. Three teams of two boys each competed in a video game. Multiple terminals were attached to a large TV screen. The game horrified me. The boys screamed, "Yes!" when the bodies on the screen exploded. I shuddered repeatedly.

Finally, I found Mark, black hair, green eyes, and glasses.

I sat quietly in a corner chair, watched the boys, and waited for the Birthday Wish.

Mark's older sister yelled into the living room and down the basement stairs, "Come on everyone, cake time."

I hurried to the dining room and waited. Mark ran into the room and threw himself into a chair. I positioned myself behind him.

The downstairs boys poured into the dining room. They were still cloaked, but yanked off their masks as they sat down. The black-haired boy reached into his pocket and pulled out a pair of glasses.

My eyes flitted back and forth. Two birthday boys? Black hair, green eyes, and glasses. Twins! Identical twins! What do I do? Twins were never mentioned in our classes at school.

Just then two birthday cakes were carried into the room and one set in front of each boy. Could I hear two wishes at the same time? What if I can't?

I felt a light breeze and Swift, fellow graduate of Fairy College, appeared and alighted on the second twin's shoulder. He turned his head in my direction. We looked at each other in complete surprise.

I breathed a sigh of relief. Swift always managed to get to class the split second before it started. He was never late, not really.

Hopefully we each had the right birthday boy. We waited.

My twin made the first wish.

"I want a new computer."

Swift's twin followed a moment later.

"I want a suit of armor with a real sword."

Just as the boys finished their wishes, the mother of the twins made a wish. A pink wish floated out of her heart and hovered in front of the boys.

"I wish that my boys would stop fighting."

I turned to Swift, "Did you see that?"

"See what?" he asked.

"That pink wish that just came out of their mother's heart. She wished that her boys wouldn't fight. Did you hear it? Did you see it?"

Swift looked at me as though I were crazy. "You are such a jokester. I'm leaving. I have another party to attend."

He vanished.

He didn't see or hear anything. What am I seeing? Am I hallucinating?

January 15

I wonder what Swift will do about finding a real suit of armor for his birthday twin. He certainly can't remove one from a museum. Maybe he'll create a copy. But a real sword is out of the question. No weapons are allowed as gifts.

I can easily urge Mark's father to consider a new computer for my twin, but I'm afraid that I can't do anything about the mother's wish. Wish fairies are not allowed to interfere in human relationships.

January 21

Although no parties are scheduled for today, I need to know if I am losing my mind.

I remembered the words of Professor Candle. "We are all wired differently. Even fairies. Pay attention to what comes to you from all realms of Creation. Be on the lookout for significant messages."

I need to find and watch children. I decided to try the park. It paid off.

Two boys skateboarded wildly through the park. They raced madly on the paths until one boy, unable to control his skateboard, crashed into a large mongrel dog. The boy and the dog went flying. The impact of the crash threw the dog off the path and onto the grass. He whimpered and licked his paw.

The boy landed close to the dog. He crawled over and patted the dog and cried, "I'm sorry, I'm so sorry."

That's when I saw the green wish. It came out of the boy's heart and hovered over the dog.

"I wish that I could take away your pain."

The dog's tail thumped. The green wish started to merge into the air, but at the last moment, before it was gone, a spark of silver luminescence edged in gold flashed in front of the boy's heart. The boy did not move. The dog looked at the boy and licked his hand.

I watched carefully. The boy was so shaken and so in the moment that he heard his own wish. He heard it! He lay on the ground, patted the dog, and got a dreamy look in his eye.

What just happened? What was that spark of silver and gold and what did it mean?

January 23

Because the day at the park had been so astonishing, I went to an elementary school to find more children. The younger grades had recess first. I heard and saw nothing. I admired the girls' outfits, but no one made a wish.

When the fifth graders came outside they immediately separated into little groups. Most of them talked and laughed and shrieked with the joy of being released from class.

A solitary boy walked to a bench, sat down, and stared at his feet. I wondered, did he not have any friends or did he prefer to be alone?

A group of boys ran up to him. He looked up with a little smile.

"Hey," they taunted. "Are the answers to the math questions scribbled on your sneakers? You think you're so smart getting all the answers right."

Just then, one of girls standing nearby turned her head. Her long dark braids gleamed in the sunlight as she walked toward the bench.

The harassment continued, "Why don't you go back to your old school. We wouldn't miss you."

That's when I saw the soft, iridescent violet wish. It came out of the girl's heart and hovered in the air.

"I wish these guys would stop being so cruel. I feel like crying."

The glowing violet color began to merge into the air around the group at the bench. One of the boys turned his head and became silent.

Then, there it was again, a spontaneous wish followed by a spark of silver and gold luminescence right in front of the girl's heart.

What is the significance of that spark?

February 1

I am very confused. Not only am I seeing wishes, but I'm also seeing some wishes dissolve into flashes of silver and gold. Over the last few days, I talked to all my fellow graduates and told them about the visible wishes.

They all laughed at me. They think I made it up.

February 8

Big day coming up
Saturday, February 11
4 Parties
Sorry about this,
Sparky

Julie's 13th Birthday
Pancake Breakfast 9:00
Sandee's Pancake House

Bob's 12th Birthday
12:00 Noon
Crystal Ice Skating Rink

Leo's 8th Birthday
3:30
305 Silver Road

Heather's 15th Birthday
Dinner and Sleepover
7:30
17 Robin Road

February 12

I'm too tired to write about all of yesterday's parties.

February 13

Little did I know about all of the wishes for love. Valentine's Day is tomorrow and little pink wishes are flying all over the place. They have interrupted my entire day. I always thought that Valentine's Day was Cupid's job.

February 21

Today, I scheduled an appointment with Professor Candle. In her early years she was a Master Wish Fairy. She worked birthday parties for two decades before she became a teacher. How many birthday wishes did Professor Candle hear in twenty years? How has she managed to stay so healthy? Her skin glows and she has enormous energy. I'll bet she followed the rules and did not indulge in party food.

March 3

The trip to Fairy College was disappointing.

"It's good to see you. Have some tea," Professor Candle said. She pointed to a table in the corner of her office.

"How is your new career? Are you busy?" she asked me.

"I love the parties," I answered, "but my schedule is packed. One Saturday I covered four birthday parties. I went from an early morning pancake breakfast party to a late night sleepover. At the last party, I nodded off and snapped awake just in time for the birthday wish."

Professor Candle snorted.

"I remember days like that. Don't worry. Being out there in the world is very different from school. Give yourself more time to adjust," she advised me.

Those were her exact words. They were not helpful.

"I know that this is different from school. That is why I'm here. I have questions that I can't begin to answer. Strange things have happened, things that were never covered in school. I have no idea what I am supposed to do or even if I am to do anything at all."

Her eyes widened.

"Tell me everything," she said.

When I told her about hearing and seeing wishes from children other than the birthday boy or girl, she looked at me, made a funny face, and started to laugh.

"Are you making this up?" she asked.

She reminded me of the day we practiced simple wishes. My partner, Rosemary, made a wish for slim legs. I immediately made her legs so skinny that she fell over. Her legs couldn't support her weight, but Rosemary quickly unfurled and flapped her wings and didn't hit the floor. Professor Candle, who was always looking for a teachable moment, lectured us on balance and moderation.

When I described in detail what happened at the parties, the park, and the school, Professor Candle realized that I was serious.

"In my twenty years as a wish fairy, I heard just the birthday wish, never a wish from anyone else. Not once. I heard the unspoken wish in the birthday child's voice. That was my gift. Sometimes, when the wish was very specific, I would see a picture."

Professor Candle paused.

"I will look into this, I promise" she said. "Remember, stay open to what the Universe is unfolding for you."

She urged me to continue my studies of the visible wishes. As if I could ignore them. They consume me.

"Everything happens for a reason," she said. "You have a special gift. Continue to focus on it. Eventually all will become clear."

When she advised me to start a special journal, I told her about my diary.

"Excellent, record everything" Professor Candle advised After that, we said goodbye and I left for home. I was on my own in uncharted territory.

March 4

I did not sleep well last night. The wishes of the past months paraded before me in full color.

"I wish that Grandpa would get well."

"I wish for a blue racing bike."

"I wish my parents would make up and live together again."

"I wish I could talk to animals."

"I wish for a snowboard."

"I wish they would stop fighting."

"I wish for purple rocket skates."

It was a long, long night.

March 8

I have spent days thinking about all these wishes. The parade of wishes was confusing, but eventually I began to see similarities and patterns. They break down into two main groups: wishes for things you can touch, play with, and utilize; wishes for things you can't touch, a change in behavior, a new way to be, a new circumstance.

I'm still mystified. Why do some wishes end in a spark of silver and gold? Why does that feel so important?

March 13

While I drank my morning tea, Jewel kept darting at me. She would appear out of nowhere and fly toward my head. Then she would disappear and fly

at me from another direction. She repeated this over and over. This was a new game and I wasn't in the mood to play.

"Jewel, what are you doing?" I asked.

"Yes, what am I doing?" she repeated.

"You keep coming at me from different directions," I answered.

Then it hit me. Could it be that the key is not the wish itself, but where it comes from? Where do wishes come from? I had never thought about it. We studied ways to hear and help wishes come true. We can be as creative as we like, as long as we don't hurt someone or interfere with the free will of a child.

Jewel landed on my shoulder and pressed her tiny head to my cheek.

"Finally, you're getting closer," she whispered

"Closer to what?" I asked.

"The heart of your quest," she replied.

I moaned. "Oh Jewel, if you know the answer, please tell me."

"I can't. It won't mean anything if I tell you. You have to solve this; this is your journey," Jewel said.

"I'm beginning to hate that word."

I returned to my diary, flipped back through the pages, and re-read the book. Nothing leapt out at me. I always hear the child's birthday wish. Luckily, I've never had a problem with that, but I have no idea where they come from.

March 14

I have returned to my clandestine practice of spying on children. I'm looking for answers to my questions.

I wandered around and found a house that appealed to me. Why was I drawn to that particular house? Because it had shiny metal sculptures in the yard. I peeked in the window. Did this house have children? Yes, the family was seated around the dinner table: a mom, a dad, two girls, and a boy.

The food didn't interest me. I had cut down on human food and increased my intake of wild foods and water from a forest spring. My complexion was smooth and glowing again and I wanted it to stay that way.

After dinner I started my investigation. The eldest daughter retired to her bedroom and experimented with nail polish. I liked the hot pink best, but she chose midnight blue. The body painting ritual fascinated me, but I had to move on.

I slipped into the boy's room, but could barely find him. He rested in a nest of dirty sweats and socks, engrossed in a paperback novel with a two-headed alien on the cover. I listened and waited. The boy was on another planet. Time to move on and keep searching.

I found the youngest child glued to the TV, watching an animated show starring a talking white stallion and two talking border collies. Their conversation seemed silly to me, but the girl loved it.

The first commercial break was loud with fast images of dolls wearing dark eye makeup and dancing to punk rock music. The show continued. The second commercial offered a stuffed toy of the show's horse.

The girl was riveted. "I love you," she said out loud to the TV.

"I wish that you were mine. I would take such good care of you."

There it was, at last, the answer. Wishes for stuff come from TV.

March 19

I have learned nothing new in the last few days.

This evening I spied on a mother and her young son. I hovered in the corner of the dining room while they ate baked macaroni and cheese with a mixed green salad.

"Did you finish your homework?" the mother asked.

"Not yet. I have to watch the news, summarize one news item, and read two chapters for English."

The mother nodded and looked out the window.

"Keep the TV low. I don't want to hear it."

"Don't you want to know if Daddy is safe?"

"We won't know it from the news. The images give me nightmares. They creep into my dreams and I see him wounded or worse. I'd rather picture him walking through that door."

"Me too," the boy said out loud.

That's when I saw the pink wish come directly from the boy's heart.

"I wish that Daddy would come home from that war and stay home!"

This time, I was riveted.

March 20

I have a lot to think about.

March 24

Luke's 15th Birthday
March 25, 1:00
68 Main Street
Sparky

March 25

I thought that all wishes for toys and stuff came from the TV, but today I learned that wasn't true. This has been an enlightening day for my investigation.

Today's birthday party was in a pizza parlor. The pies kept coming: a fried eggplant with pesto pizza, a white pizza with artichokes and feta cheese and my favorite, a mushroom pizza with lots of garlic and arugula. I allowed myself a tiny taste of each pie and waited for the birthday wish.

"I loved that scene when the bridge blows up and collapses in slow motion," one boy said.

"When the space ship landed in the park and flattened the trees; that was awesome. No one had a clue," another boy said.

Luke did not speak. I rested on his shoulder, peered down, and watched him draw a space ship in minute detail.

He finally looked up.

"I thought that the visual effects could have been better," Luke said.

His friend punched him on the shoulder, "You are such a dork. Why are you always doodling?"

Just then, the birthday cake appeared. I waited.

"I want a professional graphic pen and ink set."

I saw it. The inks came in twelve tiny bottles of vibrant colors. The pens had nibs of different sizes. He was an artist! This wish fueled his passion. Not all wishes for stuff came from the TV. I was thrilled about what I had just learned!

April 3

My schedule is packed. When I am not working, I am watching children. This includes most afternoons and evenings.

I'm tired. Is this what people mean by burning the candle at both ends?

I miss flying through the forest with my friends. I miss the fragrance of the earth and talking to the flowers.

April 7

Grace's 13th Birthday

April 8, 12:00 Noon

1010 Ulster Ave

Sparky

April 8

Today's birthday party distressed me. It started in a gymnasium where a mini tornado of girls stretched and tumbled. Their hair was pulled back in tight ponytails with stairways of hair clips confining any wayward strands. One girl kept moistening her hand with saliva and smoothing it over her head.

I found Grace stretching on a mat. Her movements reminded me of a dancer.

Her mother approached her and asked, "Grace, don't you want to practice tumbling?"

Grace grimaced. "No, I need to stretch."

"But I paid for the gym so that you could demonstrate your floor exercise routine to your friends," the mother said.

"Not today, Mom, please."

This was unusual, a birthday girl who was not interested in her own party.

A whistle blew and a voice yelled, "Five minutes."

The girls completed their routines and gathered their towels and bags. I waited while they trotted off to the showers.

I followed them to a small vegetarian café. No junk food at this party. These athletes stayed in shape.

The girls heaped food on their plates. They were ravenous. I was curious about human vegetarian food so I hid in the table bouquet and looked at all the servings.

There was a choice of a hummus and roasted red pepper sandwich, quesadillas with guacamole, sour cream and fresh salsa, or a Portobello mushroom burger with tahini sauce over wild rice. A huge bowl overflowing with spring greens completed the menu.

The food disappeared at a rapid rate.

The kitchen door swung open and I saw flickering candles. It was a carrot cake made with spelt flour and topped with a cream cheese icing.

I stationed myself behind Grace and waited, and waited. No wish. I tuned into her heart and saw a grown up Grace dancing in front of a huge audience. She was on point wearing a classic pink tutu.

"She wants to be a ballerina," I thought, still waiting for her wish.

The ballerina disappeared and Grace appeared at a gymnastics meet with a beaming mother by her side.

"I wish that I could win first place. Then she'll love me."

Her breath caught. Whoosh, she blew out every candle.

My stomach plummeted. Grace yearned to be a ballerina, but she made a wish to be a champion gymnast. This was a wish to please her mother. I didn't know what to do. I do not want to help that wish come true.

My head is spinning. I'm beginning to realize that school is just the very beginning. Most learning continues after graduation. But what am I learning?

I need to see Professor Candle right away. I'll make an appointment for tomorrow.

April 9

When I arrived at Professor Candle's office, I was stunned to see Professor Pan, the chairman of Fairy Botanical Relations. His huge hands gently cradled a tiny cup as he delicately sipped tea.

Mistress Starlight, head of Fairy College, sat in the corner spinning yarn with a drop spindle. Plants were hovering in the air, lending their color to the yarn.

"I've invited Professor Pan and Mistress Starlight to our meeting," Professor Candle said. "They are very interested in your experiences."

Professor Pan and I nodded at each other. I had enjoyed his classes immensely.

"Thank you for the message about the girl who wished to communicate with plants. I'm searching for someone to teach her," he said.

Mistress Starlight and I had never spoken, but I had often seen her flitting around the college trailing long strings of hand spun yarn. She seemed more interested in her knitting than the students. I could never figure out how she became head of the college. Why take the time to knit when a fairy can instantly create any garment?

I couldn't wait any longer.

"Professor Candle, did you learn anything?" I blurted out.

"I have interviewed all the professors. Not one has ever seen a wish the way you described it."

My shoulders slumped. They didn't believe me.

"But, we believe that you have and we want to continue this discussion," Professor Candle said.

Mistress Starlight put her yarn down and turned to face me. Her dreamy violet eyes were suddenly clear and sharp.

"Why did you specialize in children's wishes?" she asked.

The change in her startled me.

I stammered, "Because kids fascinate me. They are so unpredictable. But it's more than that; there is something about them that mystifies and attracts me."

"What do you mean?" she asked.

"I'm fascinated by them. Children are so full of life, so full of joy. When I was younger, I hid near their houses to watch them play. I love their games and their birthday parties are filled with games. That's why I became a birthday wish fairy."

"Anything else?" Mistress Starlight asked.

"I confess I started watching them again."

"Have you discovered anything?" the Mistress asked.

I took a deep breath.

"It occurred to me that where a wish comes from might be more important than the wish itself."

They looked at each other and smiled.

"In what way?" asked Professor Candle.

"At first, I thought that all wishes for toys came from TV commercials, but the birthday party at the pizza shop changed that theory."

I projected a moving vision of the birthday boy, the space ship drawing, and the pen and ink set.

"He has to have those materials. He's an artist," I said.

"Yes, it's his life's passion," Mistress Starlight agreed.

"Is it important for the children to know where their wishes come from? And does it matter in my fulfilling a wish?" I asked.

"It shouldn't," the Mistress replied. "Children often lose interest in their toys. For some, they never really wanted them. For others, it's a time of discovery."

"This wish came directly from the boy's heart."

I showed them the boy wishing his father safely home from the war.

"Wishes of the heart are very important, very deep," the Mistress agreed

"But there's more," I said.

I projected the party at the gymnasium and the wish to become a gymnast.

"What do I do with that wish? She yearns to be a ballerina. I'm so confused. I don't know what to do."

My wings drooped as I ran out of steam. I had nothing left to say.

"What do you think you should do?" asked Professor Candle.

"For that birthday wish, nothing. It's not her heart's desire. She wished it to please her mother."

Professor Pan put his teacup down and stood up. His head touched the vaulted ceiling.

"There is no law stating that you must fulfill every wish. If it feels wrong, don't do it," he said.

"And none of this explains the silver and gold spark," I said. "It's special, I know it is."

"For now, keep following your intuition," Professor Candle said. "It won't lead you astray."

I left Fairy College for the second time without any answers. But they believed me. Whatever is going on is somehow real and I must continue my search for answers.

April 11

So far, I've seen the silver and gold spark twice. When the boy crashed into the dog and when the girl was saddened by the cruelty of her classmates.

No birthday cake and no birthday wish. Both wishes arose spontaneously and both wishes dissolved in a spark of silver and gold. Why? Why am I seeing these wishes?

April 16

Today I felt a strong urge to return to the hometown of the skateboarders.

Instead of going to the park, I wandered around the village streets looking for something.

I passed a grocery store, a hardware store, and an ice cream store. I love ice cream and the temptation to wander in for a teeny taste of Super Dark Chocolate tempted me, but I continued searching. Why did I come here?

Just then, I heard a door click shut and a voice say, "That's it boy, you can do it. Let's go for a slow walk."

I turned and there was the wild skateboarder, coming out of a vet's office, gently leading a dog that had a white lampshade around his neck.

What's this? I looked closer. The dog's back leg was swollen and had a shaved area with a long line of tiny, dark stitches.

I followed them as they strolled down the street. After about five minutes they returned to the vet's office and the boy emerged with another dog. This one had a large bandage on her belly.

"Come on Cookie girl. You're getting stronger every day. You're almost ready to go home."

As she wagged her plumed tail, I heard her thoughts.

"Thanks for taking care of me. I miss my boy so much. I'm not so lonely when you're here."

The skateboarder continued. "I'm thinking about becoming a vet when I grow up. What do you think about that, girl?" Then he paused and thought to himself. "What am I doing, talking to a dog?"

But Cookie nuzzled and licked his hand. She looked directly into his eyes and I heard her inward answer. "Oh yes, you'll be great."

Is this the missing piece of my puzzle? Is the silver and gold spark related to what he becomes when he grows up?

My wings fluttered with excitement. I must find the girl with the long braids.

April 18

I returned to the girl's school and peeked into her fifth grade class. The students were divided into small groups that organized recycling projects for the neighborhood.

As the clock approached lunchtime, the teacher made an announcement.

"Remember, conflict mediation training starts Thursday at 3:30 pm. You'll learn how to listen, how to help resolve problems between people and, I hope, how to prevent violent situations from developing. Is anyone interested?"

The girl with the braids shot her hand into the air. Perfect timing.

April 22

I had been looking forward to today, but it was nothing like I expected. The carnival had come to town and I had planned to relax and enjoy it.

When I arrived, the midway surged with a huge crowd. The combined smell of hot dogs, French fried potatoes, and popcorn made me nauseous.

Because the kids love them, I wanted to experience the rides. I found an empty seat on a huge teacup and grasped the bar as best I could. It was too thick for my tiny hands and slick with sweat.

The operator pressed the 'on' button and the cup started to move. It went faster and faster and spun round and round until my hands lost their grip and I was flung out of the teacup in the direction of a ticket booth.

I beat my wings rapidly and steadied myself. Whew! That was close. I almost crashed into the booth.

No more rides for me. I'm too small. I'll try something tamer. I looked around and saw The House of Mirrors.

I swept in behind a group of girls. The mirrors made them tall and skinny, then squat and fat. The girls squealed and pushed each other to the front of the crowd. One girl bumped into me and the force of the blow slammed me to the floor.

I shook my head to clear it. When I opened my eyes the treads on the sole of a descending sneaker were inches from my face. I spun madly, beating my wings for extra speed, and rolled away to a safe spot.

No one could see me. My invisibility did not protect me from injury. I had to get out of there, fast. My flight out of The House of Mirrors was erratic. I needed a place to rest and to catch my breath.

I found a sheltered space in a display of hand woven baskets and checked myself for bruises. A large black and blue mark discolored my shoulder.

My wings fluttered anxiously and my whole body trembled. Slowly my heartbeat returned to normal.

Coming to the fair was not a good idea. My eyes were closing in the middle of the day. I decided to take a short rest before going home.

I snuggled into a basket, pulled a potholder over my body, and closed my eyes.

For a blessed moment it was quiet, then voices started to swirl in my head:

"I wish I had a strawberry ice cream cone."

"I wish that just Dad and I came to the fair."

"I wish I was in the garden instead of in this madhouse."

"I'm old enough. I wish she'd let me go on the roller coaster."

"I wish Mommy would let me help with the baby. She is so sad."

"I wish I was surfing."

Something had burst open inside me and I heard all the voices, all the wishes at the same time. I was overwhelmed and didn't know how to quiet this bombardment.

My shoulder throbbed, my head pounded, and my eyes ached.

I pushed the potholder aside, staggered out of the basket, and launched myself into the air. I flew straight into a cone of pink cotton candy and almost plummeted to the ground My wings, sticky with spun sugar could barely move.

Frantically, I looked around and saw a bucket of water. After a quick rinse and a rapid flutter, my wings were free of spun sugar.

I had to get out of here. Where should I go?

The forest, I had to get to the forest. I pictured the soothing greens of the woods, closed my eyes and whoosh, I was there, in the midst of all the trees.

My body totally relaxed for the first time in months, for this was my ancestral home.

I roamed around, listening to the conversations between the plants, the animals, and the creek.

"Stay with me," a huge oak tree invited. "I would be honored to have you as a guest."

"Thank you. I desperately need a quiet place to rest, but tomorrow I must continue my search. May I sleep over?"

"Of course. I know who you are and would be delighted to host you, for your home tree is my cousin."

I leapt high into the branches and felt the tree embrace me. I closed my eyes and fell asleep instantly. It was the most refreshing sleep I'd had in months

April 23

I awoke with a burning question. Where do the wishes that end with a silver and gold spark come from?

As I wandered deeper and deeper into the forest, the leaf canopy screened most of the daylight leaving little patches of dappled color. The symphony of birdsong lifted my heart and I kept going.

Hours later, I caught a glimpse of a silvery light. I approached slowly. The forest was different here. A huge circle of trees called to me. They were all sizes and all shapes. Some leaves were enormous and others were tiny; some trees were tropical and others were of this climate.

I had found the legend, The Circle of Elders, a place unknown to humankind. My parents had told me of the Circle, a sacred living grove that holds the planet in unity, but I never believed that it truly existed in form. How could one tree of each species on the planet exist in the same place?

"It is because we are a family," I heard the trees answer as one. "We have been waiting for you."

I grinned. Why was I not surprised?

Their welcoming energy entered my heart, my spirit soared, and I felt a glimmer of hope.

April 26

I have spent the last few days in The Circle of Elders. The ancient trees hold me in their gentle majesty. Within their peaceful presence, I am finally ready to go deeper.

Surrounded by the peace of the deep
forest, my energy expanded. I inhaled
the regal life force of the trees, the
sweet essence of the wildflowers, and
the wild free joy of the animals. I sighed
deeply. Once again, I felt my complete
connection to all of Creation.

When the sun rises, I will ask my question.

April 27

When pink and gold clouds streaked the morning sky, I flew down to the ground and landed in the exact center of the Circle. The Ancient Ones were watching.

I sat down and slowed my breathing. My eyelids dropped until just a slit of daylight showed. I waited until I could feel the pulse of the forest in my body.

"Why do some wishes end in a silver and gold spark?" I asked.

I waited.

I sensed a change in the air around me. My eyes flew open. The Circle of Elders was still there, but the tree edges had softened and a Being of Light merged in and out of every life form of the forest.

A soft lavender light appeared before me. It coalesced into the most beautiful fairy I had ever seen. Long lavender hair dusted with starlight framed her face and translucent golden wings held her aloft. My heart quickened.

"I am the Great Mother of the Fairies," she said "I have been waiting to meet you"

"But why me?" I stammered.

"I have been watching your journey into the land of wishes. You are right. The silver and gold wishes are very important. They are the most important wishes of all. Watch."

She waved her arm.

Suddenly, I saw a young man in a vet's office cleaning a deep jagged wound on a cat's shoulder. I heard the words, "He is a healer. This is who he is in Eternity."

It was the boy I had seen working in the vet's office. He was all grown up. He had acted on his wish and became a veterinarian, taking great care of many, many animals.

That picture faded. I waited.

The next vision showed a room with people seated around a large round table. A woman with a long dark braid and silver earrings introduced two groups of people to each other. One group wore modern day suits and ties in subtle shades of gray and blue while the other group wore flowing tunics and pants decorated with intricately embroidered designs.

At first they wouldn't speak to each other, but slowly the woman with the long braid led them into a conversation.

I heard the words, "She's a peacemaker. This is who she was born to be."

It was the young girl with the braids, all grown up.

"How did you do that?" I asked her.

"It's similar to showing a picture of what has already happened. You know how to do that. This time, I parted the veil of time to look ahead. It's easy. The veil is as thin and delicate as a flower petal," the Great Mother said.

"Why didn't I learn about these wishes in school?" I asked.

"These wishes have always existed, but you are the first Wish Fairy to see them. Be with this a while and learn all you can. It has been a pleasure to meet you."

She dipped into a curtsey and fluttered her wings. I felt the air shift around me. In a spark of golden light, she was gone. I didn't get a chance to thank her.

I fell into a deeply restful state. The trees hummed around me.

April 28

When I awoke, I could barely contain my excitement. The Great Mother of the Fairies; I met the Great Mother! My friends will never believe me.

Immediately after my excitement and awe in meeting the Great Mother, I realized that I had forgotten to ask the most important question. Where do the silver and gold wishes, the wishes that relate to a child's future come from? As I asked the question, I felt a huge vastness. A deep calm settled into my body. Am I getting closer to the answer? But what is it? And what is my place in this mystery?

I had been sitting for days with the Ancient Trees, bathing in their translucent silver light. I didn't want to leave The Circle of Elders, but it was time for me to go home. I launched myself up high in the air and turned very slowly, looking at each tree.

"Thank you for everything," I said.

Every leaf of every tree rustled. "Come back whenever you need us," the Trees said, "We are always here."

April 28, 29, and 30

Instead of instantly returning home, I decided to take my time. I needed to digest what I had learned.

I flew slowly through the forest for three days, stopping to rest one night with my friend the oak tree.

May 1

Jewel zoomed around my head in happy circles. She started a game of Catch Me, but I grabbed my diary and combed it for clues about the silver and gold wishes.

But Jewel would not let me read. After minutes of Jewel flipping my diary pages, I threw it down on my porch and flew after her. Of course, she outraced me and left me hovering in empty air. I tried a new tactic and went invisible. Instead of chasing her, I tried to guess her direction and waited for her. After the third try, I cupped my hands and caught her gently against my chest.

"Gottcha," I said. I opened my hands.

She landed on my shoulder.

"You're different. What happened to you in the forest?" Jewel asked.

"My life changed. I met the Great Mother and learned that some wishes are related to a child's future. That discovery resonated in my heart. I used to think that being a Wish Fairy was all about parties and games. But it's much, much more."

"Of course it is. This is your journey," Jewel said

"What is this journey you keep mentioning?" I asked.

But Jewel did not answer.

"This feels so important. A wish is such a quiet, fleeting moment, so easily forgotten. I desperately want to do something to help. But what can I do?" I sighed.

"I wish I could help children remember their silver and gold wishes."

I watched, amazed, as a pale violet cloud floated out of my heart. And then, the spark of silver and gold luminescence exploded in front of my chest. I was speechless.

The air shifted. The Great Mother appeared before me.

She shimmered as she spoke, "This is more than a wish; this is what you came to embody. This is the dream of your soul."

I felt the answer vibrate through my whole being. "Is it the same for the children?" I asked in a whisper.

"Yes," she said. "Everyone's soul aspires to something, something very special. One of the greatest challenges in life is remembering this because the soul's voice is not always heard. Sadly, some do not even know of its existence."

She flew even closer, looking deep into my eyes.

"But sometimes that voice emerges as a wish. If everyone followed their soul's dream, this would be a very different world. Letting your spirit guide your life brings great joy to everyone."

"I want to help." I said.

The Great Mother smiled and enfolded me in her wings. Love poured into my heart.

"Of course, this is who you are. Your wish came from Eternity. You came to help children hear their soul's dream. This is your contribution to our planet's unfolding."

"Whoa! You look a little wobbly," she said.

I felt as though I was standing on the top of a high peak, looking out over an endless vista of mountains an sky.

For a moment, I felt dizzy, so dizzy that I grabbed hold of a daisy stalk to steady myself.

Then a vast, calm feeling enveloped me. I wondered, "Is this what Eternity feels like?"

The Great Mother smiled again.

"Yes, you have sensed what is beyond all time," she said. "It is vast, but it can also look very small. Each person has an Essence, and when that Essence is lived, it brings them true fulfillment. It's often a simple thing, like growing flowers, fixing cars, or taking care of dogs."

"I think I understand," I said slowly.

"Good," she said.

Suddenly I heard the sound of what seemed like a thousand blaring trumpets.. The Great Mother laughed, waved her arm, and the trumpets stopped.

"Because you did not give up your quest for answers, I have a gift for you. In what way do you want to help children?" she asked.

"Oh Great Mother, I want to help them remember their soul's dream," I said.

She looked at me lovingly and said, "From now on you will be able to do that. It is who you are. I will grant you a gift. Choose it wisely. Remember, the rest is up to the children."

Her light shimmered and she vanished.

I spent the rest of the day on my lily pad watching the sun light dance on the pond. I was completely incapable of doing anything else.

May 3

I can't wait to tell the Professors and the Mistress what I discovered. I scheduled a meeting for the next day. Then I went back to the pond.

May 4

After a good night's sleep, I arrived at the College. A hummingbird escorted me to the Mistress's home. She lived in an enormous tree house. Dozens of orchids were rooted to the bark of the tree. Their scent intoxicated me.

Professor Candle, Mistress Starlight, and Professor Pan were deep in conversation seated around a small round table that held four cups and a steaming teapot of spearmint tea.

The conversation stopped as soon as they saw me.

"Come in," the Mistress said. "Have some tea. How was your time in the forest?"

"Restful, amazing, life changing. I had grown used to the human world and the frantic sizzle of energy. Thanks for the time off."

They looked at each other and exploded into laughter.

"Time off," Mistress Starlight said, "you have been spending a lot of time with people. 'Time off' is a human concept. How can you take time off from life?"

"We felt something momentous come to pass. Tell us about it," Professor Candle said. "We are all ears."

As soon as she spoke those words, their ears grew as big as their heads.

They were acting so goofy and this was serious. I couldn't wait to tell them what happened.

"There is something very special, very significant about the wishes that dissolve in the silver and gold spark. They are not the usual wishes for stuff or for things to happen. They even look different."

I hesitated. Would they believe me? I might as well say it.

"They express the deepest Essence of a child."

Mistress Starlight asked, "How did you reach that conclusion?"

I told them about the boy working at the vet's office and the girl training to become a peace maker.

"Both children made choices in their lives relating to their wishes," I said. "Now, I am certain that these wishes are related to their destinies. I saw it in the Circle of Elders."

"They told me you had arrived," Professor Pan said excitedly as he beamed at me.

"Now is the time to tell us about the Great Mother," the Mistress said.

I was surprised. "How did you know?"

Her eyes grew dreamy as she spoke. "She told me. I met her a long time ago. I will never forget that first meeting."

Then her eyes cleared. "Tell us exactly what happened."

So I did.

"When I was in the Circle of Elders, I asked about the wishes that dissolve in a spark of silver and gold. The Great Mother appeared and introduced herself. She showed me two visions, spoke to me, and then vanished."

"Watch," I said as I shared the visions with them.

"I keep wondering, why am I seeing these wishes? No one else sees them. The other wish fairies think I'm imagining things, but I don't care what they think. This feels like the most important part of my life."

I paused to see their reactions. They were smiling and that gave me the courage to continue.

"When I returned home, I had told Jewel about my experience in the forest. I couldn't stop thinking about those two visions. Seeing those children all grown up and embodying their wishes touched my heart. Then, spontaneously, I made a wish to help children remember their silver and gold wishes."

I stopped talking. My eyes filled with tears.

Professor Pan laid a gentle finger on my shoulder. "It's OK, we believe in you. Please continue. What happened next?"

"The Great Mother appeared and told me that it is the dream of my soul to work with these wishes. But what can I do? I'm a Birthday Wish Fairy."

"What do you want to do?" Professor Candle asked.

"I know that all wishes are important, but I don't want to be a Birthday Wish Fairy anymore. I want to work with the Wishes of Eternity, the wishes that express a soul's dream. To help me, the Great Mother gave me a gift, but I have no idea what it is. Do you know what the gift is?"

"No. Her gifts are unique to each fairy. You will have to figure it out," the Mistress said. "But we have a gift for you."

They stood up.

"We are pleased to announce," Professor Candle said, as a diploma edged in silver and gold materialized in front of my eyes, "that you are the first Wish Fairy to specialize in the Wishes of Eternity."

We are pleased to
proclaim you:

WISH FAIRY
SPECIALIST
in
WISHES OF
ETERNITY

Professor Candle,
Mistress Starlight,
and Professor Pan

My heart pounded and my wings fluttered. I flew happy circles around them.

"But how do I do it?" I asked.

"Continue watching the children. You'll figure out the rest. You've done wondrously so far," the Mistress said. "We do not want to stifle your creativity."

"We're very curious to see what you will do," Professor Pan said.

I went home in a daze. I have been granted a gift, but I have no idea what it is.

May 5

I checked the mirror. No messages, no parties.

I sent a note to Sparky:

> *Do I have any parties to attend?*

> *Nope, your time is your own.*
> *Sparky*

No party schedule. What am I to do?

I remembered my mother's advice, "When you have a question, broadcast it to the Universe. Sit quietly and imagine getting the answer. Then, be patient. With time and silence the answer will become clear."

May 8

How do I help the children remember their deepest wishes? What can I do?

I remembered Professor Candle's last lecture. "Do all that you can to help a wish come true, but never, never interfere with the free will of a child. They must make their own choices."

With a noticeable effort, she stopped her fluttering hands and placed them firmly over her heart. She hovered in place.

"This is a line you cannot cross. If you do, disaster will befall you. You will lose the ability to appear anywhere instantly, a party, a friend's house, a swimming hole. You will lose the gift of manifestation, the ability to create something instantly, a toy, a tool, a book, a sound."

She turned her head and looked at each student slowly, one at time. She had our complete attention.

"You will lose the very essence of what makes you a fairy. You will lose the ability to come and go at will, to communicate with all of life. You will no longer feel the web of creation."

The entire class gasped.

How do I help the children without interfering with their free will?

If I lose my fairy essence, what would become of me? I must be very careful.

May 10

I woke up with the words 'Remember, Remember' reverberating in my head.

How do I help the children remember their wishes? What makes something more memorable? For me, it's a moment that stands out in time because it's more colorful, more fun, more chocolate, more loving, more something. What will it be for the children?

I have no idea.

May 13

I keep thinking about the Wishes of Eternity. Does the Universe choreograph these special moments so that the soul's wish can arise?

May 15

As I sat on the porch and drank my morning tea, the breeze caught the wind chimes and tinkled a lovely song. Perhaps an unexpected sound would make a wish more memorable. I could make the sound of tinkling bells. That's easy for a fairy to do.

It was time to experiment. I flew to the nearest playground and waited.

The older kids were in school, but a little boy was playing in the sandbox. I watched him enthusiastically fill his pail with sand. When it was full he stood up, lifted the pail, and laughed as he emptied the sand back into the box. He immediately sat down and started to refill the pail.

After watching him fill and empty his pail three times, I knew that my timing was critical.

I flew closer. As the boy stood and lifted his pail for the next spill, I made the sound of tinkling bells. It worked. He clutched the pail to his chest and looked around. I made the bells chime again. He turned with a puzzled look on his face.

The boy stood for a moment and waited. I waited. When no other sound appeared, he turned his pail over, laughed, and watched the sand pour out.

The unexpected sound of singing bells caught the boy's attention. But would it help him remember a wish?

May 16

The sound experiment was promising. It made me think about the senses that humans depend upon: hearing, taste, touch, smell, and sight.

I couldn't experiment with taste. As much as it would work for me, it did not feel right. Too invasive.

Touch also fell into the invasive category. I don't want to startle or endanger anyone. That left sight and smell.

I called Jewel and we flew to the pond. Jewel landed on a wild rose bush that was in full bloom. The branches cascaded over the edge of the pond and the blossoms were reflected in the water.

"Why are you so quiet?" she asked.

"I am thinking about something. What kinds of smells do you like the best?" I asked her.

"The smell of bugs, especially mosquitoes and flies," she answered.

"But if you weren't hungry, what would it be?"

"I love the deep complexity of a flower's perfume. The layers of scent often stop me, even when I am dining. Why?" Jewel asked.

"How do I help children remember their wishes for the future, their wishes of destiny? I can make the sound of tinkling bells. Perhaps, at the same time, I could create a flower perfume in the air. What do you think about that idea?" I asked.

The reply came from an unexpected place.

"Let us help," the wild roses said. "We need the children to know who they are in Eternity. We need all of them. The flowers will help. You just have to ask."

Jewel and I were amazed. I hadn't thought to ask the plant kingdom for help.

"We know the hearts of all the children and which perfumes will make a lasting impression," the roses said.

"Thank you," I said.

I lounged on my favorite lily pad, closed my eyes, and began to contemplate the recent changes in my life.

While searching for answers to my questions, I discovered my destiny, the deepest wish of my soul.

I am the very first fairy to specialize in the Wishes of Eternity.

The Great Mother gifted me to help children remember these wishes. With that memory, I felt my whole body vibrate with joy. My wings fluttered and I flew a happy circle.

Everything was as it should be. I was embodying my destiny and joyously doing what I was meant to do.

Eternity and Joy. Destiny and Joy. This is it! This is the key to my gift.

I have an idea and know what to do. But is it allowed?

May 17

At first light I launched out of bed, skipped breakfast, and went to Fairy College. I flew directly to Mistress Starlight's tree house, landed on an orchid, and waited.

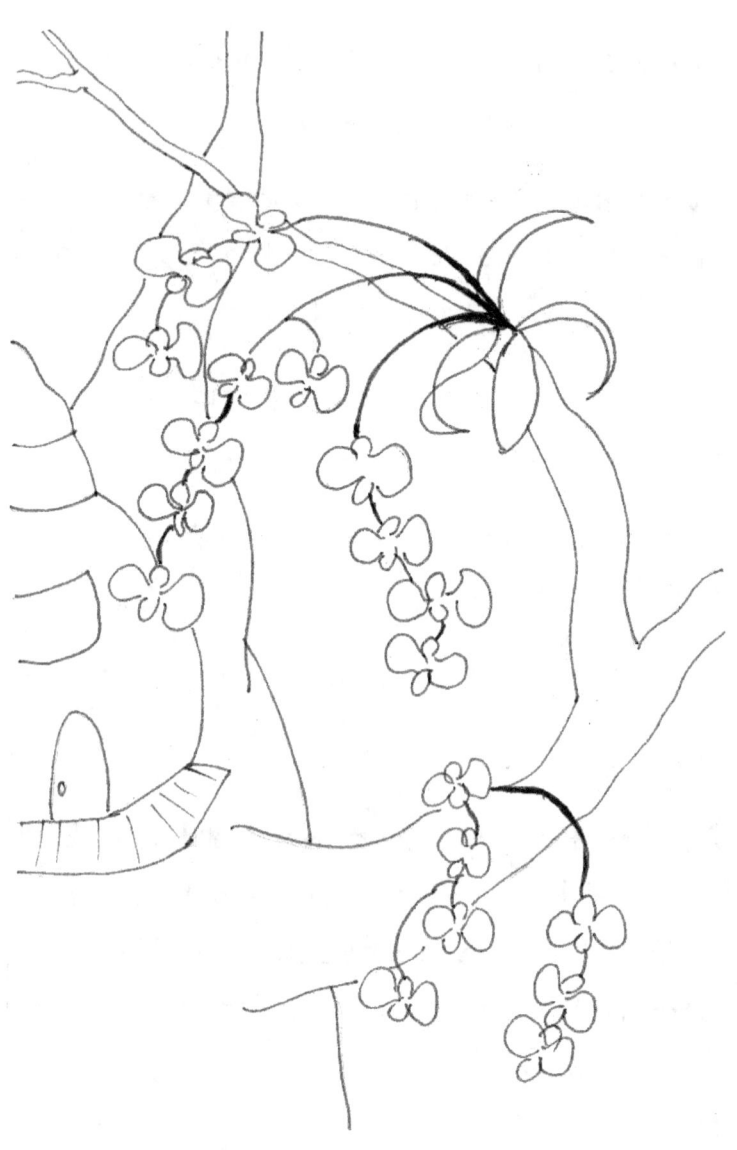

I had never come before without an appointment, but I had to speak to her. A question tumbled in my mind.

Within seconds the Mistress appeared before me. Her hair was snarled and she was still in her nightgown, but her eyes were bright and inquisitive.

"Ha! I knew it would be you," she announced. "What is it that could not wait?"

"I figured out how to use my gift from the Great Mother, but I am not sure if it's allowed," I answered.

"You know the rules. As long as you don't cross those boundaries, anything goes," she said.

She patted my head.

"You're doing fine. We have been watching you. Trust yourself."

June 3

I awoke to a hot, humid morning. Thank goodness for my silk chiffon dress. It was like wearing a soft summer breeze.

I asked Jewel if she wanted to accompany me to the forest.

She hovered in the air as she decided. Her wings were a blur.

"Yes, it will be cooler in the woods," she said.

A pale lavender haze hung over the woodland creek. We followed the water into the forest. The air was indeed cooler.

Up ahead, veiled by the mist, I saw a muted splash of red at the edge of the creek. A new flower, perhaps. I flew closer to investigate.

A boy explored the shore of the creek. His red shorts, leather hiking boots, and socks were splattered with mud. He studied everything as he worked his way deep into the woods. Nothing escaped his interest: the fish, the frogs, the plants. He even lifted rocks to examine their underside.

He shook his head and I heard his thoughts. "It's almost time to turn back. I promised to help mom with the yard, but I'd rather stay here. There's so much to see."

Something caught his eye and he plunged into the middle of the creek with his boots on! He bent over to investigate. He tugged at the edge of a large plastic garbage bag. Sodden cereal boxes, empty food packages, and plastic bottles spilled into the water.

His shoulders slumped and his head dropped. He picked up every water-logged piece of litter before it could float away.

"Not again, more litter left by campers."

His eyes filled with tears.

"How could someone leave trash in this beautiful place? I don't understand it. I wish I could keep this creek clean and all the creeks free of garbage. Then I'd clean up the oceans."

I saw the wish; it was green. It came out of his heart and started to dissolve into the air, but at the last moment, before it was gone, a spark of silver luminescence edged in gold flashed in front of the boy's chest.

This time, I was ready, ready for his wish, and ready to use my gift.

I made the sound of tinkling bells and at the same time projected the vibration of joy into his body. He broke into a surprised smile. The flowers were on time too. Suddenly, the scent of lilacs hovered over the forest creek.

I magnified the beating of his heart, flew right up to his ear, and whispered,

"Who are you in Eternity? Who did you come to be? What did you come to do? Remember, remember this moment."

His eyes opened wide and he stood very still.

I felt the air shift and looked up. There, perched on Professor Pan's massive shoulders, I could see Mistress Starlight, Professor Candle, and Jewel. They had huge smiles on their faces.

I was so stunned that for a split second I lost my concentration.

Focus, focus, I told myself.

Just to be sure I whispered again, "What is your deepest wish? Who are you in Eternity?"

The End

ACKNOWLEDGMENTS

I couldn't have completed this without support from so many friends.

For reading, discussions, and suggestions: Donna Elberg, Bruce Warren, Margo MacLeod, Mary Christopher, Cathy Yelverton, Suzanne Goddard, Nancy Whitlow, and Deeber Berk

To my beloved friends and family for their support and encouragement: Charlotte Smith, Kathleen Moga, Nanda Tuttle, Maddye Boxer-Belov, Beveraly Bellinger, Rosalie Burgher, Barbara Johnson, Mary Guiliano, Raecine Shurter, John Lucarelli, Oonaja Malagon, Andrea Pastorella, Lara Sobel, Nadine Sobel, Regina Sobel, Deborah Sobel, Prem Sobel, and Joe Ferrara

I apologize if I have forgotten anyone.

Thank you.

ABOUT THE AUTHOR

Linda Sobel lives in the Catskills Mountains of New York State with her husband Joe and her enthusiastic chocolate lab, Leo.

She is a visual artist who has given her life to Beauty, from her magnificent gardens blooming with flowers, herbs and vegetables to paintings, bead work, and clothing.

Her love of Creation propels her to write books that lead children to discover and follow their deepest paths.

"I write the books I wish I could have read as child. Had I read *Diary of a Wish Fairy* as a child, it would have planted the seed for my spiritual journey decades earlier."

Linda Sobel can be contacted at lavender4sky@gmail.com.

This is her first book.

FOR YOUR WISHES AND NOTES

MORE WISHES AND NOTES

QUESTIONS AND PONDERINGS

Have you ever had a wish arise spontaneously? What were you doing at the time? Is this activity a guide to what you want to pursue in your life? Think about this. How does it feel?

In the first August 18th party, the Wish Fairy is recognized and acknowledged for who she is and what she does. Do people see you for who you truly are? Does this feel important to you? Why?

At the December 21st Winter Solstice gathering, the Wish Fairy eventually feels a deep yearning for something unidentified. Have you ever felt such a yearning? If yes, follow this feeling and see where it leads you.

On April 7th, Grace yearns to be a ballerina, but instead makes a wish to please her mother. Have you ever experienced turning away from yourself to please someone else? If a similar situation arose, would you act differently? Why?

On May 1st, the Wish Fairy has a surprise second meeting with the Great Mother. When told about the Wishes of Eternity, the Wish Fairy is enveloped by a vast, calm feeling. Have you ever felt anything like this? What were you doing at the time? Does it feel worthwhile to seek this feeling?

Is there an adult, a close friend, or anyone that you can have a conversation with about your path in life? Sometimes it's worth stating goals out loud so the Universe hears you. How would you start?

FORTHCOMING TITLES
BY LINDA SOBEL

The Keeper of the Song
Call Yourself Awake

www.ingramcontent.com/pod-product-compliance
Lightning Source LLC
Chambersburg PA
CBHW070508260626
47161CB00004B/1495